'Twas the Night Before Summer

By Anne Margaret Lewis • Art by Wendy Popko

Mackinac Island Press

for the love of reading

'Twas the night before summer
and all through the land,
children were dreaming
of sugar beach sand.

They dreamed of adventures
their summer would bring,
of campfires and picnics,
and kites on a string.

But me, I just sat
on the edge of my bed,
thinking of boredom,
just scratching my head.

Could it be I'm too old
for summertime fun?
Had I lost all my whimsy
before summer had begun?

Would my summer drag on?
Oh, what would I do?
I sat terribly, miserably,
gloomy, and blue.

Then my window flew open.
Now how could that be?
The curtains were billowing,
calling for me.

I dashed towards the window
with caution and thrill.
I grabbed ahold tight,
peering over the sill.

Down below in the sandbox
sat my brother's toy boat,
floating 'round his sandcastle
in his handcrafted moat.

The sky had all cleared
from the day's early storm,
with the moon and bright stars
in their picturesque form.

Splish! Splash! Sparkle! Flash!
Something dashed past my tree.
A shooting star zoomed by,
could it be…choosing *me?*

"Make a wish!" I whispered,
closing my eyes.
"I wish on this star
for a summer surprise!"

"*I wish NOT* to be bored,
or stuck in my house.
I wish to explore
like a curious mouse,
like a bear on a picnic,
a cat on the prowl,
a raccoon on the hunt,
or a wily old owl."

I finished my wish,
I opened my eyes,
and there in the sand
sat my summer surprise.

For that boat in the moat
drifted up in a hover,
revealing itself as
the 'SUMMER DISCOVER!'

Its dragonfly wings
emerged soft as silk cloth,
with the gossamer sails
of a bright luna moth.

Standing there at my window
was a charming sweet bug
with her hands on her hips,
and her body quite snug.

My brother barged in
with a look of dismay!

"Don't be scared little angels,
I'm just Luna Bee May."

"I'm Luna Bee May," she buzzed.
"I'm your wish on a star.
Hear me out if you will,
for I'm not so bizarre."

That very next moment,
our jaws dropped to the ground.
A bug that could talk,
with a buzzing-like sound!?!

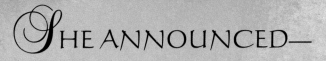

SHE ANNOUNCED—

"If you wish NOT to be bored
or stuck in your house.
If you wish to explore
like a curious mouse,
like a bear on a picnic,
a cat on the prowl,
a raccoon on the hunt,
or a wily old owl…"

"…then climb aboard now,"
said sweet Luna Bee May.
"Climb aboard now
for a grand summer day!"

We looked at each other,
in a curious way.
"We'll join your bug ship!"
we said to Luna Bee May.

We swept to the sky
on the cool midnight breeze,
slipping into the stars
above rooftops and trees.

Sand crystals shimmered
and the Milky Way sang!
"Look up to the sky,"
Luna Bee said with a twang.

"There's magic in those lights.
You must truly believe.
IMAGINE on this night,
of summer's first eve."

Summer Discover sailed on
flapping dragonfly wings,
soaring high over wheat fields
revealing wondrous things.

We paused to explore
this magnificent place,
saw squeetles and beetles
and bugs on a chase.

The Ferris wheel towered
with raspberry cars,
while we spied a new ride
called the *Dragonfly Stars*.

We dashed to the beach,
watched the ants promenade,
we rumbled through waves
of pink lemonade.

Now the fireworks boomed
as they painted the sky,
and the wind picked up speed
while big raindrops pranced by.

"Summer's here!" Luna Bee said,
"like an on-time train,
and we're not gonna melt
from a light summer rain."

My nightgown took sail
as I grabbed ahold tight
of my Luna Bee summertime-ladybug-kite.

Luna Bee chirped and cheered,
as she twittered with glee,
"Time for your big grand finale—
'The Summer Camp Jamboree!'"

"We'll toast gooey marshmallows
under the great Milky Way.
We'll sing songs of good cheer
to celebrate our grand day."

Upon this bug flying boat
we sang a campfire song.
The fire hissed and it crackled
while we all danced along.

We soon became weary
with our dark droopy eyes.
"This adventure must end,"
she said sadly...but wise.

We crawled to our tents,
went directly to sleep,
neither one of us moved,
not one bit! Not a peep!

When I awoke the next morning
with a stretch and a yawn,
magic sand filled my hand,
but the bug ship was gone.

"SUMMER SAND!" I screamed,
"sparkling green, pink, and blue!"
Then I saw a slight figure,
"Luna Bee, it *is* you!"

"I thought I was too old
to imagine and dream,
but summer *can* be great,
like pie with ice cream."

"*Summer Discover*, my dear,
wasn't just in your dreams."
"Imagination," Luna Bee whispered,
"is everything it seems."

"You're never too old
to imagine and dream.
Now your summer awaits
with a summerlicious gleam!"

$\mathcal{I}$ bounced out of bed!
I went off to explore!
No boring thoughts for me,
for it was SUMMER once more!

Text Copyright 2008 by Anne Margaret Lewis
Illustration Copyright 2008 by Wendy Popko

First Edition

Library of Congress Cataloging-in-Publication Data on file

Lewis, Anne Margaret and Popko, Wendy

'Twas the Night Before Summer

Summary: A young girl learns that you are never too old to dream and
imagine, as she is taken on the summer adventure of a lifetime by a
spectacular little luna moth.

ISBN 978-1-934133-41-5

Fiction

10 9 8 7 6 5 4 3 2 1

Art Direction and Cover Design by Tom Mills

A Mackinac Island Press, Inc. publication
Traverse City, Michigan

www.mackinacislandpress.com

Printed in China

To my parents, sister, and brothers, with whom I have some of my fondest summertime memories.

And, to my husband, Brian, who has helped show me that it doesn't take much to have fun, especially in summer.

—Anne Margaret Lewis

To my family for all of the fun summertime memories, and to my husband, Mike, for all of his support.

And a special thanks to my daughter, Ashley, for reminding me to stop and feed the ducks.

—Wendy Popko